Stories from the British Isles

Retold by Robert Hull
Illustrated by Chris Ryley
and Claire Robinson

Thomson Learning
New York

Tales From Around The World

African Stories
Egyptian Stories
Greek Stories
Native North American Stories
Norse Stories
Pre-Columbian Stories
Roman Stories
Stories from the British Isles

Color artwork by Chris Ryley
Black and white artwork by Claire Robinson
Map on page 47 by Peter Bull

First published in the
United states in 1994 by
Thomson Learning
115 Fifth Avenue
New York, NY 10003

First published in 1994 by
Wayland (Publishers) Ltd.

Library of Congress Cataloging-in-Publication Data
Hull, Robert.
  Stories from the British Isles / retold by Robert Hull ;
illustrated by Chris Ryley and Claire Robinson.
        p.   cm.—(Tales from around the world)
"First published in 1994 by Wayland (Publishers) Ltd., UK"—
T.p. verso
  Includes bibliographical references.
  Contents: Etain—Branwen—The widower Eagle—Finn mac
Cumaill—The first harp—Sir Gawain and the Green Knight—
The seal-woman.
  ISBN 1-56847-182-3
  1. Tales —Great Britain. [1. Tales—Ireland. 2. Folklore—
Great Britain. 3. Folklore—Ireland.] I. Ryley, Chris, ill.
II. Robinson, Claire, 1955– ill. III. Title. IV. Series.
PZ8.1.H883St   1994
[398.2'0941]—dc20   93-48467

Printed in Italy

Contents

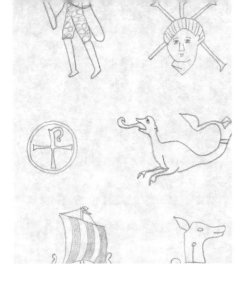

Introduction

*L*ong ago – that is how many stories begin. And long ago is when people left the huge land we now call the mainland of Europe to sail to the small islands to the west. As all peoples do when they travel, they took their stories with them.

But they also left some things behind: weapons, ornaments, drinking cups, traces of how they lived. In graves they even left joints of pork for the dead to enjoy in the afterlife. From what they left behind we know that these people, who were later called "Celts," originally lived in Switzerland, Austria, Spain, France, and in many other parts of Europe.

They settled in what are now mainland Great Britain (England, Scotland, and Wales) and Ireland. They shared Britain with the Romans when the Romans arrived. But when the Romans left and the Angles, Saxons, Jutes, and Vikings came from the east, the Celts moved over, farther west. They went to Wales, Cornwall, Brittany, Ireland, and Scotland. They took their languages and stories with them. The Anglo-Saxon newcomers had their own stories, like *Beowulf*; and the Vikings brought their stories of Norse gods and kings.

Celtic languages are still spoken. There is a Cornish language, a Breton language, and a Welsh language. There are two Gaelic languages, Scottish Gaelic and Irish Gaelic. There is also Manx, which is spoken on the Isle of Man. In all these languages, stories of the heroes and gods of Great Britain and Ireland have been told aloud for centuries. The stories are alive, ready to be written down anew in English or retold aloud in Gaelic and Welsh.

So, when children and adults read about or listen to the adventures of Arthur, king of Britain, they are enjoying stories that still come alive even though the stories are very old. Arthur and his men and horses still sleep in caves under the earth, waiting for a call to battle. Seals still change into young women, a mighty giant strides across the Irish Sea, a hero stands alone against the lord of the underworld's evil grandson.

When magical stories are told, "long ago" becomes now.

Etain

*I*nside the hollow hills of Ireland was an underworld called the Siodh. The magic beings who lived there were also able to travel in the world above.

Midir, a lord of the Siodh, leaving behind his wife, Fuamnach, once went off to visit a king of Ireland named Ailill. There he fell in love with Ailill's beautiful daughter, Etain. She fell in love with him, too, but when Midir, who was married already, asked Ailill if he could marry her, Ailill set difficult conditions. First Midir had to drain twelve huge bogs in Ailill's lands, then change the course of twelve mighty rivers. Midir went and, with the help of Aengus, the god of youth and love, he drained the twelve bogs and diverted the twelve rivers. But when he went to Ailill to claim Etain as his wife, he learned that he also had to pay Ailill Etain's weight in gold and silver.

Midir paid the price. Ailill knew that Midir, or any man, would do almost anything for Etain. Poets used to compete to describe her beauty. A poem might be sent to her in the morning that said her hair shone like sunlight on a lake, only for another to arrive in the afternoon that said it flowed over her shoulders like the most beautiful waterfall in Ireland.

But at last Midir found himself traveling with Etain toward the Siodh.

As soon as Fuamnach, Midir's first wife, saw Etain, she raged with jealousy. She immediately planned her revenge.

6

When Midir was out traveling one day, Fuamnach turned Etain into a pool of water. The pool seethed and heaved and became a shiny dragon. Then the dragon that was Etain rose into the air and shrank. Her body almost disappeared, her squeezed eyes bulged and her dragon-wings shriveled to the size of dusty blue petals. Still beautiful, Etain had become a butterfly.

Fuamnach laughed. That was as good a spell as she had ever done.

When Midir returned and could not find Etain, he suspected his jealous wife's magic. When a beautiful blue butterfly followed him everywhere and alighted on the back of his hand, Midir knew it was Etain.

Fuamnach raged again when she saw Midir by a small pond, stroking Etain's beautiful, tiny wings. She saw the loving smile on his face as Etain went dancing among the flowers at the edge of the water.

More magic was needed. Fuamnach whistled up a sudden gale, and Etain was whirled over the hills and cliffs toward the sea. She was finally driven down to cling to a thornbush by the battering waves. Salt spray soaked her wings.

For seven years Etain lived miserably near the sea, among its gray mists and salt winds. Then, one summer morning, Aengus came wandering along the shore. Seeing a particularly beautiful butterfly, he knew it was Etain. He caught her and took his prize home. He took care of Etain, keeping her in a cage of crystal and carrying her everywhere to show people.

Aengus used all his godly magic power trying to give Etain back her human shape. After hundreds of years he half succeeded. He was able to return the butterfly to her woman's form – but only during the night. During those nights he fell in love with Etain, and spent every hour of darkness with her. Every morning Etain shriveled to her butterfly form again.

When Fuamnach found out that Etain was with Aengus, she sent a fierce gale magically raging into his house, which snatched Etain up and hurled her outside, high into the winter sky. For another seven years the delicate wings were thrown about the world. A thousand times Etain nearly met her death, spiked on

thorns or drowned under waterfalls.

Finally, Etain was blown onto the roof of a castle in Ulster, the home of the great hero Etar. Falling through the smoke-hole of the castle, she landed in a strange place – a cup of mead which at that instant was being tipped into the mouth of Etar's wife.

Gulp! Etar's wife didn't even notice that she had swallowed a butterfly, which swam down into her womb and gradually changed to human form. Nine months later, Etain was born again, a thousand and twelve years after her first birth. With no memory of who she had been, she grew up a second time, as beautifully as before.

Years later, when she was a young woman once more, messengers from Eochaid, the king of all Ireland, visited Etar. It would soon be the end of Eochaid's first year as king and he was not yet married – an unlucky sign. A message went back to him that the daughter of Etar was the most beautiful girl in the whole of Ireland.

Eochaid came from his castle in Tara to meet Etain. He immediately fell in love with her, just as Midir and Aengus had done long before. Etain soon became his wife and took part as queen in the feasting and celebrations at the end of his first year as king. All the other heroes and leaders of Ireland came to Tara, and they and their wives agreed that the king's young wife was so beautiful that she might be one of the immortal gods herself.

Soon, in the underworld of the Siodh, Midir heard stories about the new queen. Could it be the young woman whom Fuamnach had turned into a butterfly so long ago? He decided to go to Tara and see for himself. When he arrived and saw her, he knew it was Etain. He was overwhelmed with love for her again and wanted her back.

Etain was someone else's wife, but he still asked her to run away with him. "You are really Etain. My Etain. Long ago the magic of Fuamnach stole you from me. You are really my wife, the true wife of a lord of the Siodh, a ruler in the underworld. Come back to the Siodh with me."

Etain laughed. "I've heard many strange things in the world but that is the very strangest! I don't remember

you. And anyway, I am wife to the king of all Ireland. I have all I desire."

Midir left. A while later he returned to Eochaid's court and challenged the king to some games of chess. Eochaid was supposed to be the best chess player in Ireland.

They played several games. Eochaid won them all. As a forfeit Midir paid him fifty swords with gold shafts, then fifty white cows and their white calves, then fifty rich cloaks. Eochaid went on and on winning, and commanded Midir, as Ailill had done long before, to perform great labors. Midir had to cut down seven forests, then make seven causeways over bogland. He did all that in a day, then returned to the castle to continue the match.

And so they played the last game. After winning so many games, Eochaid had become careless. Midir won this final one. He leaped up triumphantly and demanded his prize: "And now I claim as my reward, King Eochaid, one kiss from the mouth of your beautiful wife."

With a scowl, Eochaid agreed. "Very well. In a month's time you can come here and claim your reward. Not before."

On the day set for Midir to claim his reward, Eochaid surrounded his castle with hundreds of warriors. No one would be able to force his way into the great hall of the castle. And no one did. But, as Eochaid sprawled there in his chair, amused at how clever he had been, Midir materialized from behind a beam of sunlight that fell through the smoke-hole. He walked calmly past the feasting heroes and their wives to where Eochaid was sitting.

"Now, Eochaid, I want the kiss I have won."

Eochaid had no alternative but to ask his wife to pay his debt to Midir.

She stepped forward and waited. Passing a chain of gold over her head and holding her by the waist, Midir kissed her slowly on the mouth. As he did so, there flooded into her mind all the memory of her past life, and of who she really was.

"Will you come now?" Midir asked.

"Yes," said Etain.

10

The next moment Etain felt the weight of her body grow less. Her skin turned soft and feathery, and her neck wavered and lengthened and grew even whiter. The same changes happened to Midir.

Before the eyes of the amazed men and women at the feast, Etain and Midir gradually discarded their human shape and grew white feathers and long, curving necks. Beating their wide wings they ran along the floor of the hall, then soared up to the roof and out through the smoke-hole.

Outside the castle, warriors on guard saw two swans rise through the air and turn their outstretched necks in the direction of Midir's Siodh in Bri Leith. Glittering faintly in the moonlit night hung the gold chain that bound Midir and Etain together on their journey home, as it would on all their journeys.

Branwen

ong ago, a Welsh giant named Bran was king over all the island of Britain. He was called Bran the Blessed, because Britain was contented and prospered under his rule. He liked traveling around the country to see his people. He also liked entertainment; he was so fond of music that he took his musicians with him when he traveled, carrying them on his huge back.

Bran had a brother, Manawydan, and a very beautiful sister, Branwen. Like Bran they were the children of Llyr, the old god of the sea. Bran also had two half-brothers. One was Nisien, who was well known for bringing peace to fighting armies and making quarreling men become friends. The other was the evil Efnisien, who was just as well known for the opposite reason.

One day, when Bran was staying at his court in Harddlech, he was enjoying an hour sitting on a rock by the shore, talking with Manawydan and Nisien and some of the members of his court. He loved being near the sea and at Harddlech he slept by it. He always slept outside because there was no castle big enough for him to enter.

It was a breezy day, with the sky so blue and clear that you could see for miles. As Bran was gazing to the horizon, he suddenly lifted his hand to shade his eyes. "What do I see over there? Masts and colored sails! One, two, three…thirteen ships!"

At first the others could not see what Bran saw, but in a few minutes they too made out the tops of masts rising over the horizon, with brilliant flags streaming in the wind. "They come in a friendly spirit," Bran said. He had seen that the first ship had a glinting battle-shield held high above the deck, with its base pointing up, a sign of peace.

Men of Bran's court ran to meet the boats. A courtier came to tell Bran that the ships came from Ireland, bringing the king of Ireland, Matholwch, and a large gathering of friends, family, warriors, servants, dogs, and horses. "Matholwch has come, sir," he said, gasping after his hard run, "to say that he wishes to have the great king Bran as his ally and friend. He has come to ask if Bran's sister, the beautiful Branwen, will marry him and be his queen."

Bran roared down a welcome. "Come and feast with us. We are pleased you have come."

So the ships were pulled up on the shore, and all the people and animals stepped onto the land. There were so many of them that every farm and homestead between the sea and the mountains were needed to provide beds for the courtiers, stables for the horses, and kennels for the dogs.

That evening there was a feast in Harddlech Castle. Pigs were roasted; salmon were baked in honey; and gallons of ale and mead were drunk. Everyone, old and young, danced and sang. Bran strolled outside, often looking down into the great hall where Matholwch met Branwen and Branwen met Matholwch. She thought he was handsome and gentle; he knew she was the most beautiful and intelligent woman in the world. Bran was pleased. A marriage was arranged, and the feast grew even noisier. Just hours after the king of Ireland set foot on the great sands of Harddlech, everyone was celebrating the wedding of Branwen and Matholwch and the new friendship between Britain and Ireland.

Everyone but Efnisien. People used to say that he could make trouble between two pans in a kitchen.

Riding alone down from the mountains, Efnisien saw lights flickering in the castle. He came nearer and heard the music of harps and voices and the stamp of dancing. He reined in his horse to listen. Others were enjoying themselves. He was outside,

out in the cold, hostile moonlight beyond the
noise and warmth.

As he rode into the yard a groom ran to take the
bridle. "What's all this noise and nonsense?" Efnisien
wanted to know.

"Haven't you heard, sir? The king's sister, she's
marrying the king from over the water."

Efnisien froze with resentment and anger. He felt
no gladness for Branwen, only fury that he had not
been consulted. But he would show his brothers that
in future they should take notice of him.

Efnisien asked the groom where Matholwch's
horses were stabled. The groom told him they were
in the castle stables and the fields nearby. "Good,"
said Efnisien.

Taking care to avoid Bran, who had
grown weary and stretched out
around his favorite bay a mile
from the castle, Efnisien
rode to the fields where
some of the horses
were sleeping. He
dismounted, a
knife glinting
in his hand.

Throughout the night, Efnisien committed one vicious crime after another, cruelly and carefully mutilating all the horses belonging to Matholwch, first where they stood quietly in the dewy fields, then later where they slept in the stables. They were no longer any good as the king's horses.

Next morning Matholwch soon learned of the terrible maiming of his horses. He was full of great anger, but there was also disbelief in his mind, and shock and grief. Who could commit such brutal acts? He wept for his wounded horses and could hardly bear to look at them.

Matholwch said that they would return to Ireland that same day. He would take his new wife, but there could be no more speech with Bran.

When Bran saw Matholwch leaving, without taking leave of him or even telling him, he sent a messenger to find out why. Learning the horrifying story of the maiming, he flamed with anger too. He sent a message to Matholwch to say that he would recompense him for his loss. He said that for every horse that had been mutilated, he would give Matholwch another equally fine horse. He would also give him a rod of silver and a plate of gold.

Bran watched from the cliff as the messenger ran down to the ships, which were being made ready to leave. For a while the work of unfurling the sails went on, then it stopped, and soon the messenger returned, saying that Matholwch and a few followers would return to the castle.

They did, and again Bran greeted Matholwch. But though the king of Ireland had returned, he had not brought much speech or cheeriness with him. Bran saw that he must offer the king greater recompense.

"My lord, the evil done to you still offends you. So you must take with you to Ireland my most precious treasure, the Cauldron of Renewal."

Matholwch nodded slowly as he listened. That would put things right. The Cauldron of Renewal brought back to life those killed in battles. Dead warriors, thrown into the huge iron cauldron for a night, came to life the next morning. Although in their second lives they had no speech, their bodies were renewed for fighting.

"I am satisfied, Bran," Matholwch said. "That is a great gift."

Some of Matholwch's good humor came back to him. The great cauldron was swung on board the largest ship, and into the rest went the horses and the gifts of gold and silver. A few days later, Matholwch left for Ireland with Branwen.

For a while Branwen and Matholwch lived contentedly. A son was born to them, whom they called Gwern. But the evil thoughts sown by the maiming of the horses grew in the minds of the people. Like a slain warrior stepping from the Cauldron of Renewal, a dead bitterness came to life again.

The people began to despise Matholwch. By returning with Branwen, Matholwch had overlooked a terrible disgrace. The gifts were bribes to make him forget. "What weakness!" people thought.

Matholwch was humiliated by his people's mockery. And for no fault of her own, Branwen too found herself despised and hated. She was made to work in the castle kitchens, doing everything from peeling potatoes to washing dishes and scrubbing the floor, and she was no longer allowed to use the main rooms of the castle.

This was a terrible humiliation for Branwen, but also a great insult to Bran. To prevent him from finding out, Matholwch banned all trading ships and coracles and all boats ferrying cattle and people from crossing between Ireland and Wales.

For three years Branwen saw no one outside the kitchens, and no one discovered her punishment. Her husband pretended that Branwen didn't exist, and her son had no idea where she had gone.

But Branwen fought back.

One morning, a starling flew in through the open window of the kitchen and perched on a draining board. She threw it a piece of bread. The starling hopped forward, pounced on it, and flew away. The same thing happened the next morning and the next. In a week the starling was feeding from her hand, and it would sit on her shoulder, chattering

and whistling out of sheer friendliness. One morning, as she chattered and whistled back at it, she noticed that its whistles sounded like hers.

When Branwen heard the starling imitate her whistling voice, she realized how she could escape. "Branwen is a prisoner…Branwen is a prisoner," she began to say to it, over and over again. In a week or two the starling began to say something like it. After months of saying "Branwen is a prisoner" to her starling, its voice repeated her words perfectly. "Branwen is a prisoner…Branwen is a prisoner," the small bird chirped cheerily.

It was time. Branwen took the starling to a window of the castle facing east and released him. Off he flew, out over the sea.

A few days later, a farmer near Harddlech heard a cheery voice saying, "Branwen is a prisoner, Branwen is a prisoner." Up on the roof of his barn was Branwen's friend, telling all Wales about the misery of Bran's sister.

Bran himself knew of this within an hour, and within two hours his ships were being made ready to leave. The great Bran was too huge to fit in any ship, and the next day he could be seen wading across the sea toward Ireland, with his ships swaying along around him.

When Matholwch's swineherds saw Bran in the distance, they hurried to their king to report that a mountain had risen from the sea and was coming toward Ireland. Matholwch knew who the mountain was and prepared for Bran's coming. He would try to calm Bran's anger.

First Branwen was released, then Matholwch offered to make Gwern, who was his son and Bran's nephew, king of Ireland instead of himself. In addition the Irish people said they would build a great castle to house the giant Bran.

Peaceful Bran agreed to Matholwch's suggestions, and at first all seemed to be well. But some warriors of Ireland hid in sacks of flour in the castle, intending to kill Bran. The ever-suspicious Efnisien found them in their hiding places and had them killed. Terrible fighting then began, and went on, and on, and on.

A quicker end would have come to the fighting if Matholwch had not possessed the Cauldron of Renewal, from which his dead warriors again and again sprang to fight and wearily fight again. Then, one dark, cold, wintry afternoon, there was no one left alive to throw the dead into its renewing waters. The dead lay where they had fallen.

All the Irish were killed, including Matholwch. So fierce had been the fighting that only nine from Britain remained alive. One was Bran himself, but the great giant-king had received a fatal wound in his foot, from a poisoned blade.

They sailed back to Harddlech. When Branwen stepped onto the sands of the island of Britain she gazed around in despair. Because of her, because she had married, two peoples had been destroyed. The grief of it was unbearable. It overwhelmed her. She left Harddlech and wandered over mountains and by lakes and rivers. In a few weeks she came into Anglesey. By the banks of the Alaw River, her mind broken into pieces, she sat down and wept until she died.

"Branwen is a prisoner, Branwen is a prisoner," somewhere in Wales chirped a cheery starling. Until his voice, too, fell silent.

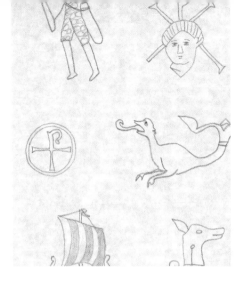

The Widower Eagle

What are the most ancient beings to live in the world? It was by chance, a long time ago, that the answer was discovered.

In the woods of Scotland lived a sad old eagle. He and his mate had lived together for many years, and in that time many eagle children had flown off to take possession of forests and crags through all the island of Britain. Now the eagle mother had died and Eagle was sad and lonely. He didn't want any more children, but he did want another mate for company.

Since there was no other eagle of his great age, it would have to be a different kind of being. Eagle had heard of a very old creature, Old Owl of the North. Perhaps she could be his mate? Eagle wondered if she was old enough. Was she a being as aged as himself, and too old to have children? Eagle, the most noble of the creatures, did not want his superior blood mixed with that of any creature less noble.

I had better ask, Eagle thought to himself. *I shall ask a creature older than I am about the age of Old Owl of the North.*

So Eagle went to Stag of Rhedynfre, in Wales, and asked how old Old Owl of the North was.

Stag said, "Eagle, do you see this leafless, dry, old oak stump? I remember when it was an acorn, high out of my reach. Then it became an oak sapling and for three hundred years it grew and grew. It was a great, full-grown oak for three hundred more years. Then for

three hundred years it decayed until it died. After death it will be three hundred years returning to the earth; sixty of those are gone already. I have seen all these years and Old Owl of the North has been old all that time. But I know no more than that. To discover truly how many years she has lived, you can ask a friend who is much older than I, Salmon of Llyn Lliwon."

Eagle went to Salmon of Llyn Lliwon and asked her if she knew the age of Old Owl of the North.

"If you count the number of scales on my body, and add to that the number of speckles on my scales, then add the number of grains of spawn which I contain, that is the number of years that I have lived. And when I was young, Old Owl was already old, and none of my friends heard anyone mention the youth of Old Owl. But a friend of mine, Ouzel of Cilgwri, may know her age for sure. Go and ask him if you want to be certain."

Eagle went to Cilgwri and found Ouzel perched on a small piece of iron. He asked Ouzel if he knew anything about the age of Old Owl.

"This piece of iron can be picked up by a child," Ouzel said, "but when I first perched here it was a great anvil. No work was done on that anvil except that I sharpened my beak on it. It has been worn down only by the sharpening of my beak on it night and morning and by the brushing of my feet and wings on it as I alight from that thornbush. I have done this for so many years that my memory cannot hold the thought of them, and for all those years Owl was old, and her children and her grandchildren were old

hags past the time of bearing children."

So Eagle saw that he could marry Old Owl of North Britain. He need not fear that with her he would have children less noble than himself.

The second courtship of Eagle taught the world precious knowledge. It was through the courtship of old Eagle that the oldest creatures in the world were discovered. Only ridges of rock are older than Eagle of Scotland, Stag of Rhedynfre, Salmon of Llyn Lliwon, Ouzel of Cilgwri, and Old Owl of North Britain.

They were the most ancient beings to dwell in the world in the very beginning of time.

Finn mac Cumaill

*F*inn mac Cumaill – sometimes called Fingal – was the son of Cumaill, leader of the Fianna, or the Fenians, as they were also called. They were a legendary band of warriors whose amazing exploits are the subject of many stories told in both Ireland and Scotland.

When Cumaill, the chief of the Fianna, was killed in battle by his rival, his wife feared for her life and fled to the woods. There she had a son, Finn, and to keep him out of the clutches of Cumaill's enemies she left him in the care of two women. One was a druid, Bobdall, and the other, Fiacal, was a warrior.

By the time he was six Finn was as strong as a young man and possessed the skills of a hero. The two women taught him to run by chasing him day after day through the woods with a stick, until he was quicker than smoke in a wind. They taught him to swim by throwing him into the river, again and again, until his body slipped through the water as easily as the shadow of a cloud.

But in time, Finn mac Cumaill, wanting to see something of the world, ran away from his stern teachers. He lived first among poets and learned by heart long poems with great wisdom in them. Then he worked for a year in the forge of a smith, where he made a sword for himself. Finally he decided it was time to journey to the sacred city of Tara, the home of the Fianna. He arrived in time for the feast of Samain,

the time when summer ends and winter begins the new year. At this season, the doors of the Siodh are open and there are no barriers between the world of light and the underworld.

All kings and chiefs were welcome to feast at Tara during Samain, but the young Finn was not yet a king or chief, and he was also a stranger. But his bearing was that of a hero, and as soon as he said, "I am Finn, son of Cumaill," he was able to enter the great hall and eat and drink with the rest. He watched kings deep in talk, servants going back and forth with gold dishes and jugs, dogs wrestling for bones. He gazed at beautiful women and the quick hands of harp players. And yet this feast seemed to be too quiet for a celebration, a feast without real joy. He noticed that as the evening wore on the talk grew quieter, the music sadder.

The Chain of Silence was shaken and the talk and music stopped completely. Conn, the High King of Tara, spoke: "Fellow kings and friends, you know that tonight Aillen will come again. In a few hours, unless we prevent it, these walls and timbers will blacken in the searing flames he carries. Some of us will die. Which of us then will prevent it? Who will preserve Tara against Aillen, the wraith of fire?"

There was no need to shake the Chain of Silence again. None of the heroes spoke. One stared into his wine as if his courage were drowned there, another pulled at his beard, another drew his finger around the rim of a cup.

Until he heard Conn's words, Finn did not know of the terrible thing that had taken place every Samain for nine years past. Aillen mac Midna, grandson of the lord of the underworld, emerged from the dark below the world to attack the holy city of Tara. Each year he attacked with flame, but first Aillen sent harp music as soothing and quietly beautiful as the murmur of lake waters in summer. The music swirled over the land, lulling all the listeners into deep sleep, then Aillen hurled fearsome blue fire into the city and broke its walls, causing terror and death. Each year Tara had been rebuilt; but now, again, the city awaited Samain with dread.

That was what caused so shameful a moment of

hesitation. It was ended when Finn stood up. "I am Finn, son of Cumaill. I will face the music and then the fire of Aillen, provided that due reward comes to me after my victory."

A hundred stupefied faces gazed at Finn.

"All that I can give I will give," said Conn.

It was enough for Finn. Out he strode into the dark, past the flickering torches, over rampart after rampart, until he stood under the stars. Fingers resting on his sword-handle, he listened to the noises of the night, straining for a hint of the wraith's approach. The night was totally still, but Finn's hearing, trained for years on the smallest scraps of sound, made out the restless shifting of reeds at the lake's edge, the scurry of a rat across mud, the stab of a heron's beak. From the silence around these few sounds he knew that the wraith had still to make its first move.

"Finn mac Cumaill!" a voice whispered behind him from the dark. Finn whisked round, but the figure emerging from the dark was an old warrior who spoke as a friend.

"Many years ago your father saved my life. This spear will save yours." The spear that the old warrior offered Finn was wrapped in a sack.

"Why is it covered?" Finn asked.

"It is dangerous. Uncovered, it aches to fly like a hawk from the hand. This famished steel pursues its prey with the hunger of a falcon after a long fast."

"What is its name?"

"Its name is Birga. It was forged by Lein, the smith of the gods. He beat the fire of the sun into it, and the power of the moon. Its head is hammered to the shaft with thirty rivets of Arabian gold. Your father took it from Aillen. It is Aillen's own spear that waits to find him out. But do nothing until the music steals across the dark plain like a mist. Then press the cold steel against your cheek. You will not sleep then. Soon the music will fade, and Aillen will make ready to hurl his breath of blue fire. At the first sight of flame you must take aim. Then be ready to gather the flame in your cloak, and release Birga."

"And there is nothing else?"

"Only one thing. Be prepared, when you uncover

25

Birga, for your head to swim. Birga has been
hurled into a hundred horrors and the stench
of the past hangs around it. And now I must go.
I dare not hear one note of the harp of Aillen."

With that the old warrior turned and went.
Finn heard his footsteps fade, then he faced
the dark again.

He did not have long to wait. Ten times softer
than a faint whisper in the reeds came the
first tremble of harp strings. A single note
grew and spread till it was a mist of shimmering
sound. It was as if, from the dark in front
of him, every reed and grass blade, every
creature and every pool of quiet
water poured its own murmuring
earth-music through the
strings of Aillen's
appalling harp.

Finn felt himself listening, wrapped in chains of sound. He felt himself entranced and slipping over into sleep. With a surge of panic he uncovered Birga and clasped the blade to his cheek. There was an overwhelming smell of decay that made him feel sick, then his head cleared and the spear quivered in his hand like a living thing.

A thin strand of moon glimmered in front of him and faded. Then another. And another. Finn realized that he was looking at moonlit harp strings and that the drifting mists were Aillen's cloudy, white hands moving over the strings.

Nearer and nearer the wraith came. Finn could now see the outline of the whole body. He could make out a great head, pale as a slug's, with a dark well of a mouth. As he watched, the dark red jaws pulled open wider and from them poured a torrent of green-blue, crackling light. It came surging toward Finn, writhing and leaping like a mountain stream in flood. Finn pointed his spear at the hissing light and spread his cloak wide. The flames found the tip of the spear, and a fierce, blue-white light roared and foamed along it, shaking Finn's whole body, then writhed down into the folds of his cloak. Dying flames ran here and there, merging into each other, and went out. Only a few thin shreds of fire fell to the ground, flickered, and died.

Finn hurled Birga. It screamed from his hand towards Aillen, who was already hurrying back in a trembling fuzz of gray light toward the entrance to his underworld. Birga reached Aillen before Aillen reached safety. The last thing Aillen saw was the welcome green light of the underworld filtering from the opening doorway. Then the green light faded.

Aillen had made his last raid on Tara. Finn found Aillen's body and hacked off the head as proof of what he had accomplished, then set off through the dawn to claim his reward from Conn the High King.

And so it was that Finn mac Cumaill gained the leadership of the Fianna.

28

The First Harp

In all parts of the world, there are stories that explain how certain things came into being. The discovery of music, one of the most mysterious of human inventions, is sometimes described as accidental, as in this story from Ireland about the first harp.

A long time ago, the poet of the gods, Coirpre, quarreled with his wife, Canola. She ran away from him and lived alone by the seashore.

One morning she was sitting on a rock gazing out to sea when the murmur of the waves was joined by another sound, gentle, swaying, quiet, and musical. It gradually sent her to sleep.

Behind the rock was the skeleton of a whale, and the sound came from the wind drifting through the bones and hanging sinews and across the long, swaying needles of baleen that hung in the cavern of its mouth. The whole frame of the whale jangled gently.

Coirpre saw the whale as he came along the beach, and the next moment he discovered his wife sleeping. He had traced her footsteps to this seashore, and as he saw her again he heard the strange song made when fingers of wind touched the whale skeleton.

Coirpre found a beautiful, curved piece of driftwood. Taking a knife from his belt he cut some of the thinnest sinews and strips of baleen from the whale and fitted them into the frame of driftwood. He drew his hand across the thin fibers. A beautiful rippling sound came from them, like water spilling over stones.

Coirpre drew his hand over the strings. Soon, Canola was dreaming that she and Coirpre were drifting across a lake that rippled in the noon sun. After a while she awoke and saw Coirpre. They put their arms around each other.

And that is how the first harp was discovered, and how Coirpre and Canola came together again.

Sir Gawain and the Green Knight

Arthur was the legendary king of Britain who founded the Knights of the Round Table. The tasks of his 150 knights were to bring order and quiet to any land they passed through, to put right grievous wrongs, and to protect the weak. To do all this they often went on perilous quests, like the one that Sir Gawain undertakes here.

It was New Year's Day at Camelot. Outside, the snow poured across the land. In the warmth of the hall, the lords and ladies waited for the feast to begin. But King Arthur himself – such was the custom – could not join the New Year's feasting until a marvelous tale had been told or a fine fight had taken place between a noble knight and a stranger. There was no stranger at court, so a tale would have to be told before he could eat a morsel of the fabulous feast.

The first course was brought in, with a great flourish of trumpets and a din of drums and pipes: fish, broth in great silver bowls, beer, and wine. The lords and ladies waited to begin. The next fanfare sent them all to their food, all except Arthur, who was waiting for a tale. He gazed around, wondering who would tell it.

A marvelous tale did begin, but it was not told from anyone's lips. As the echoes of the trumpets faded, a horseman burst through the outer door and into the hall. With a terrible clatter of hooves, the rider reined in before Arthur.

31

A terrifying sight confronted the king. The rider was taller than any man he had ever seen, huge and square across the shoulders and chest, narrow at the waist, and long-legged. Men and women were astonished at his size. But his size was not what terrified them. Every part of him – hair, flesh, fingernails – was green.

Green hands, green eyebrows and lashes, long green curled hair with streaks of gold, thick green beard. The Green Knight gazed at the silent court. He wore a long green cloak with a fur hood. He had green hose on his huge legs and green shoes on his feet. A green belt went around his waist, embroidered with silver-green butterflies. To add to the horror, his horse was also green. As it impatiently shook its green head, its mane of green glinted where it was twisted through with gold, and a green-gold bridle jingled gently in the awful silence.

The Green Knight had no knightly armor on; he carried no sword or spear. All he held was a huge ax, which had a green shaft and a hammered blade a whole yard wide of gold and green steel.

He glared around him. The glittering court was as still as the frozen land outside. Without a word of greeting, the Green Knight said, "Who governs this gathering? Who will speak?"

Arthur sensed that this was the New Year's marvel. Here was the tale to be told before them.

"Welcome, knight! I am Arthur, king of this castle. Dismount, feast with us, then tell us your purpose here."

"I shall not linger in this hall, sir. I come in peace and carry no arms. My helmet is at home, with my sword and shield. I crave no combat among the boys without beards I see here. I've come to play a simple Christmas game. I offer my ax to whoever will hurl it at me here, in this hall, if a year later he will come and offer himself to me for a stroke in return."

He twisted around in his saddle, glaring up and down the hall to see who would step forward. No one moved. No brave knight was brave enough.

The Green Knight laughed. "What's this? At the great court of Arthur no knight comes forward for a grim little game?" He laughed again.

32

Arthur moved forward. "Sir, hand me the ax, and let us begin. Your challenge is foolish, like your laughter, but I accept it."

Watching all this, the knight Gawain knew he could not allow Arthur to risk his life in a foolish game. The Green Knight was a strange being, a marvel, and perhaps he could not be despatched with a mere blow. Gawain stepped forward.

"Let me take up this mad challenge, and shield you from danger. Of all those gathered here, mine is the life that, if lost, would be missed least."

Arthur looked for a moment into the eyes of his favorite knight, then courteously accepted. The ax was Gawain's. He swished it through the air in a few practice swings that whistled terrifyingly.

The Green Knight asked Gawain, "What is your name?" Gawain told him. In return Gawain asked how he could find the knight, to receive his return blow, should the Green Knight survive Gawain's one swing of the huge ax.

"I shall tell you when you have dealt me your worst blow. Now, shall we begin?"

Gawain stood stroking his hand along the blade. The Green Knight knelt low in front of him. He put his hands under his long, curling hair, and tossed it forward over his head, leaving his neck bare. Gawain gripped the ax hard and lifted it as high as he could, pushing his left foot forward for balance. The ax came down in a smooth swish straight through the flesh, and struck the floor of the hall a shuddering blow. The Green Knight's head fell from its neck and went rolling among the feet of the nearest spectators, who drew back in horror. Those with no room to step back prodded the hideous head along the floor with their feet.

Blood spurted from the kneeling knight's neck and spilled down the bright green of his tunic, but he did not fall, or even falter. He rose to his feet and strode after his own head as if he had dropped a coin that rolled around the room. Bending down at the feet of a group of panicked courtiers, he took it by the hair. Then he strode majestically across to his horse, and grasping the bridle hauled himself into the green and gold saddle.

33

He twisted around and held up his head by the hair so that it faced Queen Guinevere on the throne. The eyelids opened and the mouth spoke: "To fulfil your promise, Gawain, you must journey next New Year's Day to the Green Chapel, and there wait for a return blow by the Knight of the Green Chapel. That is my name. I am well known. Ask for me, and you shall find me."

Without another word the Green Knight put spurs to his horse's sides. Its hooves struck sparks from the flint cobbles of the entrance and the dangling head jolted noisily against his armored thigh.

There was a moment of terrible silence, then voices broke out in astonishment. Arthur was shaken and amazed, but he and Gawain were determined not to seem alarmed. They joked with each other about the marvelous sight they had seen, and one or two other knights laughed nervously.

The ax was hung up and the feast started in earnest. Until nightfall there was such music and drinking and dancing that most lords and ladies forgot how afraid they had been. Not Gawain. Brave though he was, he did not forget for a moment.

The months passed. On the morning of All Saints' Day Gawain spoke to Arthur. "I must be gone tomorrow, as winter begins again, to prepare for the trial God has granted me."

Arthur, saying nothing, embraced him. He knew that Gawain must go.

The next day, Gawain was dressed in costly steel armor. Everything shone like the moon, and it was all hinged together and secured with nails of red gold. Under the cold, clanky armor he had fur and soft cotton clothing, and over it a rich cloak.

His horse, Gringolet, was almost as richly armored and dressed as Gawain. Gringolet was also in steel, with new gold nails and red cloths.

Gawain was nearly ready. He was handed his glittering helmet, studded with gems and padded on the inside. He kissed it and crammed it over his head.

"Good day to you all," was all he said. And away he rode.

Many of the courtiers gazing after him thought it a waste that so splendid a knight should submit to the rules of such a grim game. "And that knight in green was a coarse, unearthly fellow," they said. "No one invited him to our feast, no one asked him to contrive such a murderous combat. It would be better if Gawain had stayed among us and led us with his example here at Camelot."

But Gawain had given his promise.

Gawain rode north, through wild hills and valleys. He had faith that he would soon meet someone who would tell him the way to the chapel of the Green Knight.

But he met no one who knew; neither swineherd nor peasant nor friendly knight had heard of the Green Knight or his chapel. Alone he fought wolves; alone he battled with wandering wild men; alone he rode against ogres and giants.

And so he went on until Christmas Eve. Gawain was cheerful as he rode under trees white with frost, where rooks cawed in the cold sun. Eventually, shimmering through the oak wood, a huge castle came into view: tall, chalk-white chimneys, battlements, and turrets; immense, sunlit walls towering up from a dark moat.

Gawain rode up to the drawbridge and shouted "Good morning!" A porter pushed his head out of a window. "Will you say to your lord that a worthy knight seeks lodging?"

"Wait a moment, sir" came the reply, and the head disappeared into the castle.

Pulleys creaked as the drawbridge was lowered. A door opened in the great gate and a few curious men and women pushed through to watch Gawain ride over the bridge and dismount. Gringolet was led off to be stabled.

The lord of the castle stepped forward to greet Gawain. He was a huge, broad-shouldered figure, a man of enormous strength. He welcomed Gawain generously. "Knight, you must stay here as long as you wish. Treat everything here as your own."

"My best thanks to you, lord. Riding through this icy morning, I never thought to stand next to a blazing fire and hear such warm words."

"It is our pleasure. A youth will look after you."

Gawain was guided to a sumptuous bedroom with rich curtains and hangings. His mud-splattered armor and his own stained clothing were exchanged for rich garments of silk and ermine. Soon he was being entertained in the great hall with music, wine, and delicately prepared foods.

Gawain lingered at the castle through the time of the Christmas feasting, until there were only three days left before his encounter with the Green Knight.

He spoke to his generous host: "Lord, tomorrow I must take my leave. On New Year's Day I must meet the Green Knight. I have only three days to find him."

The lord laughed. "You need only three hours. His chapel is two miles from here. You can ride out on New Year's morning and still not fail your meeting. Remain with us. I shall hunt during the day, but you can stay quietly in the castle, preparing your mind for the ordeal."

"Very well, and my best thanks."

"There is one thing," the lord said. "I want us to make a friends' bargain. I promise that whatever I win in the hunt I shall offer to you at the end of the day. In return you must promise to offer me whatever you win or gain here."

"Of course," said Gawain, with a laugh, "though what I can win here except a few innocent games, I do not know."

They drank a glass of mead to their bargain, and embraced like true friends.

Next morning, the lord went to the hunt, while Gawain stayed behind with the knights and the beautiful women of the court, including the most beautiful of them, the lord's wife. He had a few moments walking alone with her and was able to ask her hurriedly, "My lady, can I serve you as your true knight in this coming ordeal? Will you agree to be my sovereign lady and rule my heart?"

"Yes, and yes," she said, and gave him a single kiss.

When the lord came back at the end of the day, he showed Gawain the deer he had killed. "It is yours," he said. "Now, what have you won in this house today?"

And Gawain embraced the lord, kissing him on the cheek as if in greeting.

The lord looked uncertain. "It would be better if you used words to tell me what you have won," he said.

"That was not our bargain, my lord," replied Gawain.

"In truth it was not," the lord said with a laugh.

On the second day, Gawain's lady, the lord's wife, walked with him through the castle grounds, listening as he talked about the death that seemed to be approaching him. To comfort him she gave him one kiss as they walked out and then another as they returned. At the end of the day Gawain embraced the lord twice, in return for the savage boar he had killed.

The third day was the last that Gawain would be able to spend in the company of his lady. It came to the time of parting. He wanted to take a simple gift to remember her by, and asked for a glove. It was too poor a gift, she said. Instead she offered a gold ring. Gawain refused; it was too rich a gift. And so she gave him a scarf of green silk.

"Take this," she said. "Anyone who wears this scarf is safe from all evil. But you must reveal to no one who gave it to you, no one." Gawain wanted to take the scarf and yet he thought he should not. But the lady of the castle pleaded and pleaded with him, and finally Gawain accepted the scarf. And in farewell, also, he received three kisses from her.

When he met his host that evening, Gawain embraced him three times. His host had hunted all day and had only taken a fox. Gawain's third gift was a poor fox-skin.

New Year's Day was clear and frosty. With a servant to guide him, Gawain set out on Gringolet. They journeyed together for a mile or so, then the servant reined in his horse.

"I will go no farther," the servant said. "The path to the Green Chapel leads only to death. Noble knight, you should not perish this way. If you would only abandon this hopeless quest, I will never tell a soul, on my word."

"I cannot," said Gawain. "Better my body should perish than my sacred honor."

"So be it, my lord," said the servant, and he showed Gawain a stony track next to a stream coiling under grim cliffs. Small waterfalls sprayed off the summits, and ravens called over the frozen trees.

Gawain rode on alone. Soon, rounding a turn in the track, he saw in front of him a moss-covered mound. He dismounted, hitching Gringolet to a tree.

At one end of the mound there was an opening. Gawain went in. The inside of the mound was a huge, damp cavern, its clammy walls hung with moss. But he had only just begun to inspect the strange chapel when a terrifying sound rang through the cave. It came from behind him, from outside, a ghastly, shrill sound of stone scraping rhythmically on metal.

Gawain knew what the sound was before he saw what made it. On the opposite side of the stream stood the towering figure of the Green Knight. His long shadow reached across the stream to Gawain's feet. The knight was sharpening a long-bladed ax on a grindstone. Watching the sparks fly, Gawain shivered. Then he shouted: "I have come to take the blow you promised me!"

The Green Knight looked up. He laughed and held down the blade for a few more shrieking turns of the grindstone. Then he strode down to the stream and, putting the ax-handle on a rock, vaulted over.

"So. You have come. Let us begin. Take off your helmet and kneel to receive your payment."

There was no point in trying to delay or escape. Gawain did as the Green Knight instructed him, and in a few seconds, heart thumping, was kneeling in terror at his feet. The knight lifted his ax high in the air. Gawain saw the shadow of the ax start to fall toward him and clenched his shoulders, shuddering.

The Green Knight stopped the ax in midair. "Surely this is not the fearless Gawain who kneels here, flinching away from the blow and shaking with terror. The Green Knight did not flinch."

"I shall not move, sir. I shall receive the blow. Have no fear."

The Green Knight laughed and raised his ax again. "Well then, good luck, Sir Gawain. May your noble knighthood save your neck." And he laughed again and started to swing down the ax. Gawain saw it coming, and this time held his body as stiff as a tree-stump.

But the ax was again arrested in midair. The torture being inflicted on Gawain maddened him. "Strike if you will! No more stalling and stammering!"

"Very well!" And in a terrifying flash the ax aimed at Gawain's neck came whistling all the way to the earth, shaking it like thunder on impact.

Gawain was hit. Glancingly. The flesh on his neck was nicked, and blood spilled onto his shoulder. He must have been killed, he thought, but somehow he was still conscious. Perhaps he had already entered some afterlife. Then he felt for his head. It was still on! In a mad surge of happiness he leaped up, dragged out his sword and shouted, "Enough! One blow was all I had to take!"

But the Green Knight was smiling. There was no more rage in his gaze, only courtesy and respect. "Enough, sir. You have been paid the blow due to you. You did as you pledged you would do, though not entirely, and I have repaid your actions, deed for deed."

The knight's words puzzled Gawain: "Why do you say 'not entirely?'" But as he spoke, a thought came to him. The Green Knight was a huge, broad-shouldered figure, but no more so than the lord of the castle!

"That green silk scarf you wear belongs to my wife. Yes, the Green Knight is also the lord of the castle. My wife tried your strength of heart just as I did. With my knowledge she caused you to love her for a while, and with my knowledge gave you on the first day one, and on the second day two kisses. You and I promised to give the other whatever we won. For two days, in return for my gifts, you gave me in friendship the same number of kisses my wife gave you. For that honesty I twice stayed the ax. But on the third day she also gave you the silk scarf, and that you concealed from me. For that secrecy you received the harmless blow that only cut your neck like a careless stroke of your own razor."

The Green Knight, the lord of the castle, smiled at Gawain. Gawain could not smile back. He was confused and angry. He tore off the green scarf and threw it toward his opponent. "Take the treacherous thing! I never want to see it again, or the owner of it!"

"Come, Gawain, it is time to take up our friendship again. Come with me back to my castle and improve this cold New Year's Day with some feasting. Keep the silk scarf. It was a true gift. And you can learn to talk easily to my wife again, in open friendship, and leave loving behind you. Come."

But Gawain was not in a feasting or friendly mood. A game had been played around him, and he felt a sharp guilt for having lied to his host. His host had forgiven him, but he could not yet forgive himself.

"No sir, thank you. I will go my own way and ponder on what has happened. And thank you, I will keep the green silk scarf, to remember my weakness by."

And Gawain went on his way.

The Seal-Woman

*T*his story of a "seal-woman" is from the Scottish Highlands. In parts of Scotland there was a belief that seals were fallen angels. There are many stories in which seals turn into humans.

A young farmer named MacCodrum was beachcombing one morning, walking along the edge of the sea looking for objects that had been washed ashore. He wanted a good piece of wood for his barn, the kind with useful iron bolts still embedded in it.

Toward midday he sat down for a rest, leaning back against a rock and watching the sunlit bay. Suddenly he saw a glinting, dark shape bobbing in the waves. It was the head of a seal. Then there was another, and another. They were coming ashore.

The seals squirmed across the wet sand to some rocks near his, without seeing him. In a few moments he wondered if he was dreaming. One after the other, they peeled away their sleek, black skins and were no longer seals. They were beautiful women instead, who went racing back into the sea to swim and splash in the noon sun.

MacCodrum watched them. One of the young seal-women was even more beautiful than the rest. She had the most musical soft cry and was the quickest and most graceful swimmer. He slipped behind the rocks to where the sealskins had been left. Sure enough, one of them had a deeper, more silky black sheen than the others. He thought it must be hers.

As he watched her in the waves he fell in love with her movements, her hair, her voice. Then a thought crossed his mind. If he took away her seal-clothing she would have to stay on the land with him.

He gathered up that shining sealskin and started back toward the rock. But the seal-women had seen him and came running out of the waves. They slipped into their skins and became their seal-selves again, hurrying down into the water and out to sea.

They had all left except one. The seal-woman whose skin MacCodrum held in his arms waited on the beach for him to give it back. She pleaded, "My skin is no use to you, but I cannot return to the sea without it. My home is in the depths of the waters, not here on land."

MacCodrum was saddened by her pleading, but he would not give back the skin. He knew he was making her homeless but he was crazed with love, and selfish. He turned and walked along the shore toward his own home. She followed, a long way behind, crying pathetically and calling to him to give her back the furry skin.

MacCodrum only called back, "Come home with me instead." He decided where he would hide the skin when he came to his farm. When the seal-woman finally crept, exhausted, into his yard, MacCodrum no longer held the skin in his hands. He had hidden it in his small barn.

The seal-woman realized she was in MacCodrum's power. When he asked her to stay with him she could not refuse. The only way she could ever get back to the sea was by finding her seal clothing.

And so, because it was her only hope of eventually escaping to the sea, the seal-woman stayed with MacCodrum and in time became his wife.

She only began to forget her sea home when her children were born. When she sang to them late at night she was at peace. When she played with them among the rocks near the sea, she had no desire to be anywhere else. She could sniff the salt air and listen to the steady roar of the waves without feeling despair and longing.

But at other times, especially as the children grew older, a great sadness came over her. The music of the

44

sea became unbearable. In her nostrils the salt air called and called terribly. She longed to explore again the great underwater rocks and the dark green caverns. She wanted to lie out on white ice in the winter sun.

MacCodrum guessed at her silence, thinking it must be homesickness for the sea world. He decided to hide the skin in a safer place. When the next corn was harvested, he hid the skin in a haystack. It stayed there until the following spring, when the hay was needed for the cattle. Then MacCodrum brought it into the barn again, until the next stack was built.

One morning in late spring, the children came skipping into the kitchen. They had been playing in the barn, helping their father bring in the hay, and carried on chattering away about their games. Their mother wasn't really listening, but she suddenly heard the words "beautiful coat of fur." She stopped what she was doing.

"And why wouldn't our father let us try it?" the youngest girl was saying.

"What's that?" their mother asked.

"Oh, nothing. Our father has a beautiful fur in the barn but we couldn't play with it."

"A fur in the barn?"

"Aye, up in the rafters. But he wouldn't even let us stroke it."

Next morning, when her husband was out in the fields, the seal-woman went to the barn and found her seal's clothing. When she touched it again her body shuddered with longing for the sway of the waves. As she brushed the pieces of straw away it shone as lustrously as before, like the sea under a full moon.

She put it back in its hiding place and went to call her children. They came into the kitchen and she took the youngest on her knee.

"I'm going away for a little while, children, but I'll be back and you'll want for nothing. There'll be plenty of bread and fish. So be good to your father. Now, go and play."

Off they ran.

She went to the barn and took down the furry skin. She walked over the fields to the sea. She sat on a rock, ready to dress herself and become a seal again.

45

She looked out to sea, thinking of her children and her husband. Even with freedom in her hands, she was imagining her children's voices. Then, out in the glittering bay, she saw small, silky heads and backs turn and flash.

In a few moments she was a seal again with the others, hurling herself through the clear waters under the waves, out to the open sea.

Her husband realized what had happened when the children told him that their mother was going away for a while. She had gone back home.

MacCodrum spent many days and moonlit nights wandering along the shore, hoping for a glimpse of her. He knew he would recognize her, even among a crowd of bobbing seal heads. One morning he saw a seal come ashore with a fish in its mouth, making a crying sound as it went writhing off over the sand. He knew that it was his wife leaving food for her children.

He knew that he should not have taken her from her home. One day, when the wind was strong and the waves thundered, he shouted aloud, "Forgive me for taking you from the sea. It was wrong. Please forgive me." Then he said it every day.

After that, the seal came every day to the rocks near his house and left fish there. He told his children that eventually their mother would come home. After a while he began to believe it himself. He believed it most when he heard what sounded like a voice singing above the roar of the waves, like a mother singing to her children.

Notes

Arthur (pp. 5, 31, 32, 33, 36)
A legendary king of Britain who founded the Round Table, a body of knights who went around the country righting wrongs. The story of Arthur might have been based on a real British king or hero.

Baleen (p. 29)
Sometimes called "whalebone," baleen is the long fibers or plates that, instead of teeth, hang from the mouth of certain whales.

Britain (pp. 4, 12, 13, 31)
At the time of these stories, Britain was the island that now includes Scotland, Wales, and England.

Camelot (say Kam'-a-lot) (pp. 31, 37)
The site of King Arthur's palace and court. One tradition says that Camelot was at what is now Cadbury Castle in Somerset, England.

Coracles (p. 17)
Small round boats made of animal skins stretched over a wicker frame.

Druids (say droo'-idz) (p. 23)
Priests, teachers, judges, and doctors. Druids had to learn legends, stories, poems, and many secrets of nature by heart.

Ermine (p. 38)
The white winter fur of the stoat.

Fianna (say Fee-an'-ah) (pp. 23, 28)
A warband of 150 chiefs.

Gaelic (say Gay'-lik) (pp. 4-5)
Two separate but related languages, used in the Isle of Man, Ireland, and Scotland.

Gawain (say Guh-wain') (pp. 31-42)
King Arthur's nephew and one of his favorite knights.

Mead (pp. 13, 38)
A wine made of honey and spices.

Ouzel (say oo'zuhl) (pp. 21, 22)
A blackbird.

Samain (say Sov'-ain) (pp. 23, 24)
The Celtic festival of the New Year, held on the 1st of November. The mounds of the Siodh opened and beings could pass from one world to the other.

Siodh (say Seed) (pp. 6, 9, 11, 24)
The Hollow Hills where the people of the underworld lived, who were sometimes called Faery.

Further Reading

Briais, Bernard. *The Celts.* Myths and Legends. North Bellmore, NY: Marshall Cavendish, 1991.

Clare, John, ed. *Knights in Armor.* Living History. San Diego: Harcourt Brace Jovanovich, 1992.

Garner, Alan. *A Bag of Moonshine.* New York: Delacorte, 1986.

Hastings, Selina. *Sir Gawain and the Green Knight.* New York: Lothrop, Lee & Shepard, 1981.

White, T. H. *The Sword in the Stone.* New York: Dell Publishing Co., 1978.

Williamson, Duncan. *Tales of the Seal People: Scottish Folk Tales.* New York: Interlink Publishing Group, 1992.

Yeats, William Butler. *Fairy Tales of Ireland.* New York: Delacorte, 1990.